Enchantment in the Garden

For Martha

A Red Fox Book

Published by Random House Children's Books
20 Vauxhall Bridge Road, London SW1V 2SA

A division of The Random House Group Ltd
London Melbourne Sydney Auckland
Johannesburg and agencies throughout the world

5 7 9 10 8 6

First published in Great Britain by The Bodley Head Children's Books 1996

Red Fox edition 1998

Printed in China

THE RANDOM HOUSE GROUP Limited Reg. No. 954009

ISBN 978-0-099-64441-5

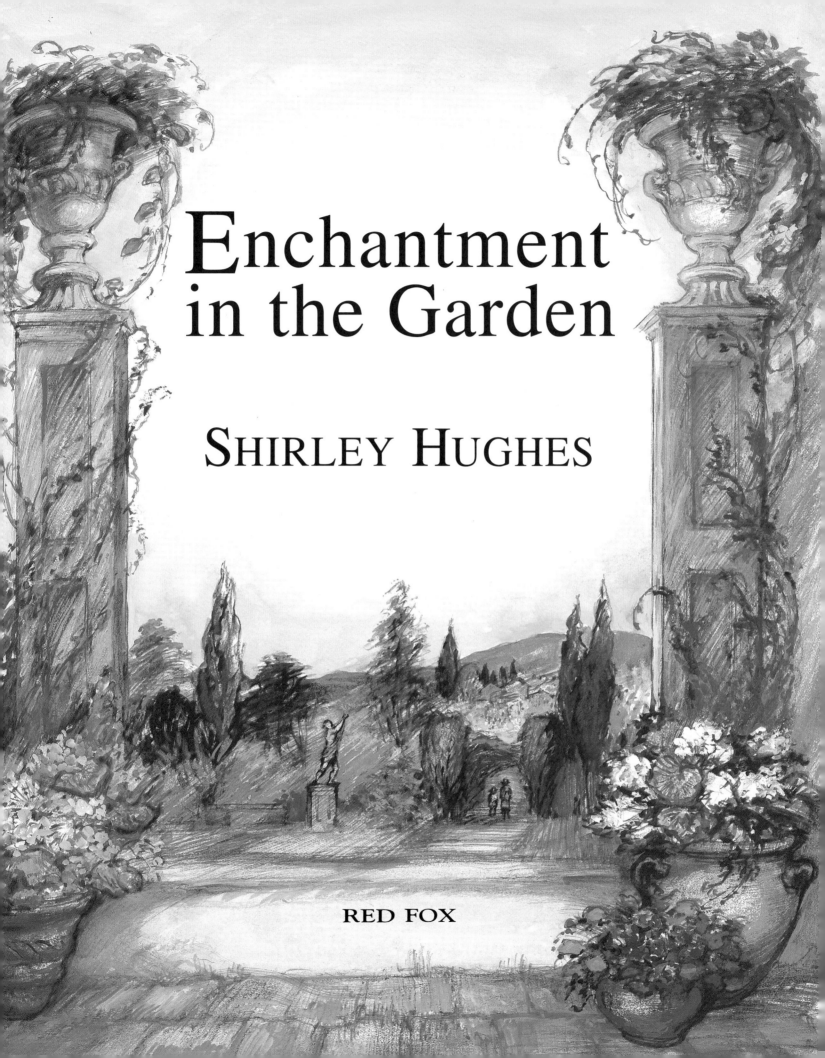

Enchantment
in the Garden

SHIRLEY HUGHES

RED FOX

Once, in an old Italian city, in a house with many rooms, there lived a girl called Valerie. The front of the house faced severely on to the street. At the back, balconies overlooked a shady garden with stone seats, a goldfish pond and plant pots overflowing with flowers.

There was also a smaller house where Pietro, the gardener, and his wife, Maria, lived. And beyond that, over a high wall, lay a great public garden which had once belonged to a merchant prince. It was full of statues. Valerie could just see some of their heads from the balcony of her bedroom.

Valerie's father was a rich
man. He owned hotels and
restaurants all over Italy and
was often away from home.
Her mother was a beautiful
American lady. She breakfasted
late, long after Valerie had
started her lessons, then drove
out to meet her friends. In the
evening she put on an elegant
dress covered in sparkling
beads and went to balls and
parties.

IN between whiles she spent a lot of time lying on the sofa in the lofty salon. Sometimes she and Valerie had tea together and played dance records on the gramophone.

Valerie was an only child. She was too serious for her age and had more toys and dresses than she could possibly need. But she had few friends and, of course, she was lonely.

EVERY day in the late afternoon, Valerie and her governess, Miss McKenzie, set out for the garden – through the cool gravel walks then out by the sunlit lake where Neptune, the great sea god, rode on a sea monster surrounded by nymphs.

Valerie's favourite statue of all was a beautiful long-haired boy who rode on a dolphin. Clear water poured from its open jaws. When Valerie gazed at them, how she longed to take off her clothes too and splash about in the lake. But Miss McKenzie would never have allowed it.

One afternoon, when Miss McKenzie was sitting on one of the stone seats with her eyes tightly closed (she could sleep sitting bolt upright), Valerie slipped away.

THE gardens around the lake were empty. The boy on the dolphin stood alone. Valerie climbed on to the curved wall which ringed the water and put out a hand to stroke his cold cheek. Then she put her face close to his ear and whispered: 'You are my best friend. I love you and I am going to give you a name.' And she sprinkled a little water over the boy's head. 'I christen you Cherubino,' said Valerie, solemnly.

The boy looked back at her. She thought she saw a dancing spark in his carved eyes.

THE next day when Valerie and Miss McKenzie arrived at the gardens, they found a small crowd gathered near the lake. The dolphin was there as usual. But the boy was gone.

'Stolen!' cried the park keeper. 'Thieves! Vandals! Someone has been in the night and taken one of our valuable statues!'

The crowd murmured angrily and the police were summoned. Miss McKenzie, tut-tutting, hurried Valerie away.

VALERIE ran ahead of her, dodging through the maze of walks. She desperately wanted to be on her own. But when at last she thought she was out of sight, she heard a scuffling behind the hedge, keeping pace with her. The sound of bare feet. She could see something moving behind the leaves. She had a sense of being watched; as though the statues were stealthily turning their eyes to look down at her. She ran faster.

Now she came to an open space. And there, suddenly, into a shaft of sunlight, stepped Cherubino! He was holding out his arms to her and laughing.

'Cherubino! You're alive!' cried Valerie, as she ran forward to clasp his hands.

There was no time to say any more. Miss McKenzie came hurrying in from another entrance and then, what a fuss! You never saw such a commotion. A boy in the gardens with next to no clothes on. Whatever next?

PEOPLE came running. They covered Cherubino with scarves and coats and hustled him away, scolding and bombarding him with questions.

Nobody paid the least attention to Valerie as she ran behind, pulling Miss McKenzie with her and shouting out: 'But he's Cherubino, I tell you! He's one of the gods of the garden!'

No one could decide what was to be done with Cherubino. A search was made for parents or relatives, but none could be found. When he tried to explain that he was more than two thousand years old and had been carved out of Greek marble, naturally, nobody believed him.

In the end, they took him to an orphanage and put him in the care of the nuns, in the hope that he would be cured of telling such wicked lies.

THE orphanage was on the
other side of the city. There
was no garden, only a gloomy
yard with high walls, where the
sunlight hardly ever ventured.
They cut off Cherubino's hair
and dressed him in a uniform;
a grey cotton shirt and clumsy
black boots like the other boys.
He was given a narrow iron
bed in a bleak dormitory and
he no longer laughed. Very
soon he fell completely silent.

No matter how hard they tried, the nuns could not get him to eat the black bread and watery stew they provided. After some weeks Signor Duro himself, the chief governor of the orphanage, had to be summoned. He quickly came to the conclusion that Cherubino was wilfully fading away.

MEANWHILE Valerie, usually such an obedient and even-tempered child, was creating a terrible fuss. She too refused her meals and lay on her bed weeping. Several expensive doctors were summoned. But all Valerie could say was: 'We must find Cherubino!' At last her mother, seriously worried, made inquiries as to the whereabouts of this mysterious boy.

PIETRO was given orders to bring the car round and drive Valerie and her mother across the city to the orphanage. They found Cherubino standing in line with the other boys. His shoulders drooped pathetically, as though the weight of his braces was too heavy for him, and his cheeks were pale and thin.

When Valerie saw him she let out a cry of joy, flung her arms around him and refused to be separated. So it was that Valerie's mother offered Cherubino a home.

IT was arranged that he would come and live with Pietro and Maria, who were childless, and learn to be a gardener's boy. As soon as he was settled and could see Valerie every day, Cherubino's health improved.

HE began to eat ravenously and his cheeks became rosy and brown from working out of doors. To everyone's delight he turned out to be a natural gardener. Seedlings prospered and flowers bloomed under his hands.

He worked hard, became cheerful, high spirited and hilariously merry. He drove Pietro to distraction, but the cats loved him.

OFTEN he and they put on a great show for Valerie, who watched giggling from her balcony. He always finished with an elaborate bow to a wildly enthusiastic, imaginary audience.

At this time, rich children were not supposed to become friendly with servants. Miss McKenzie certainly would not allow it. But in the evening, when the governess was listening to her wireless set, Valerie climbed down from her balcony to meet Cherubino.

Hidden behind the shadowy vines they whispered and laughed together and, more often, talked seriously until late into the night. Little by little Valerie learned Cherubino's story. How, thousands of years ago – even before he had become a statue – he had been alive in the morning of time. His father was a sea god who ruled the ocean, with the strength of all the tides in his limbs and forked lightning in his beard. He had fallen in love with Cherubino's mother, a human woman, and she had brought Cherubino up in her own country; a beautiful fertile place, rich with fruits and golden grain, in what was now called North Africa.

But then Valerie, remembering her geography lessons with Miss McKenzie, fetched her atlas and showed Cherubino that this part of the world was now dry desert, where only goats and camels could find enough to eat. At first he refused to believe it. Then he flew into a terrible rage and ran off.

He climbed over the wall and disappeared into the gardens. They could not find him for two whole days.

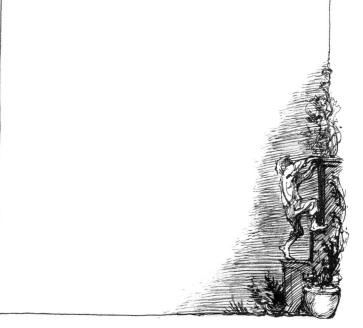

AFTER this, Cherubino became restless. He still worked hard at helping Pietro, but he no longer wanted to laugh or fool around, or talk with Valerie late into the night. He spent his spare time sitting perfectly still by the little pond, glaring at the goldfish gliding to and fro under the lily leaves.

When Valerie asked him what was wrong, he only muttered: 'The sea, the sea! I must go to the sea!' Under the suntan he had become quite pale with desperation.

The weather was growing hotter and hotter. The city was becoming unbearably dusty. By midday all the grown-ups lay prostrate behind closed shutters, to avoid the sun's fierce, wide-open eye.

VALERIE's father owned one of the largest and most splendid hotels on the Italian coast. Valerie's mother always took her there for a month in the summer. Somehow, Valerie persuaded her to let Cherubino come too.

Of course, there was the usual great production of packing and preparation before they boarded the train for Porto Azzurro.

C HERUBINO seemed to pass the journey in a daze. He only roused himself when the train began to enter a series of long tunnels, punctuated by brilliant flashes of light, tantalizing glimpses of sunlit beaches and clear green water. The sea – at last, the sea!

PORTO Azzurro was the
smartest resort on the whole
Italian Riviera. Their hotel was
a great white palace, set among
palm trees and lush foliage, its
domes and pinnacles melting
into the blue haze.

At the steps to the main entrance, Cherubino stopped. He stood stock still and refused to move. A shadow crossed his face. Only Valerie noticed.

While Miss McKenzie was fussing with the luggage, Valerie slipped over to Cherubino's side and took his hand. 'Let's go down to the sea!' she whispered. And together they ran.

THEY reached the paved esplanade and looked down on a beach, alive with people. Cherubino stood and watched them. He was as still as the statue he had once been. 'It's the sea, Cherubino – aren't you glad to see it?' asked Valerie.

Cherubino looked at the polite waves lapping on to the sugary sand. He did not reply.

INSTEAD he let out a wild cry of anger and pain. Then he was off, kicking up sand, skidding through carefully laid picnics, trampling on wet towels, sending hats, sandcastles and sunshades flying. 'Come back! Come back!' called Valerie. But she knew it was hopeless. She watched Cherubino run out of sight, then walked back alone to the hotel and waited furiously until bedtime.

But Cherubino did not return.

THAT night the weather changed. A great storm broke. Forked lightning and thunderbolts cracked across the sky. Towering waves pounded and raked the esplanade, throwing deckchairs and beach umbrellas about like matchwood.

WHEN at last morning came, the sky was still dark and threatening and a strong wind blew in relentlessly from the sea. There was still no sign of Cherubino. Now everyone began to be worried. A search party was organized, but Valerie was not allowed to join in. Her anger at Cherubino had turned to a terrible anxiety. She waited alone in the huge, glass-fronted winter garden of the hotel, staring out at the rain which fell as steadily as her tears.

The search went on for three days. In the end it was declared hopeless. Cherubino had run away they said, or perhaps even been drowned. Some of them seemed to be more irritated than sad.

V ALERIE'S mother ordered the luggage to be re-packed. The weather was so bad there was little point in staying, she said.

'But what if Cherubino comes back to the hotel, trying to find us?' asked Valerie.

'They'll let us know. You mustn't fuss, darling,' was all her mother answered.

Back in the city, the grown-ups were out of sorts and Valerie was miserable. She missed Cherubino more than she could say and wandered around the house and garden fretting over what might have happened to him.

Weeks passed.

Then, one night, Cherubino came back.

EVERYONE in the house was asleep, when Valerie was woken by tiny pebbles thrown against her shutters. She crept out on to her balcony and saw Cherubino standing there in the hot, still garden. The moon was making shadows ripple all over him like water.

VALERIE was joyful when she saw him. She slipped quietly downstairs and out of the garden door.

'Cherubino, where ever have you *been?*'

'To the sea, of course,' answered Cherubino, clasping her hands tightly. 'But – oh Valerie; it's so different from what I remember – so changed! All those hotels and villas and *motorcars!*'

'They are there so that people can enjoy themselves,' Valerie told him.

'But people don't *own* the sea any more than the fish who swim in it do,' said Cherubino. 'They shouldn't be so greedy. That's why I made the storm,' he added, carelessly.

'Don't be *silly*, Cherubino,' whispered Valerie. 'Boys can't make thunder and lightning and things of that sort on purpose.'

Cherubino plunged his hands into the pockets of his ragged trousers and drew himself up proudly.

'I can,' he said. 'I am not a boy, remember. I am the son of a sea god and I am thousands of years old! I was inside the statue until you rescued me. But now I have come to say goodbye!'

This made Valerie's eyes fill with tears, but she was too brave to cry. Instead she told Cherubino, all in a great breathless rush, about her own plans. How she did not intend to grow up like her mama and spend all her time dressing up and going to parties. Instead she was going to study all the mysteries of the oceans.

'Wait for me…stay here until I'm older…then we can explore the wild seashore together – you and me!'

But Cherubino shook his head. 'I have to go now!' he said. 'I was the god of the garden, but now I must follow my father and be a god of the sea. I must guard the wild places. And I will walk in the country where I was born, which has become a dry desert, until it is green and fertile once more!'

'THEN I'll never see you again,' said Valerie, very quietly.

'Oh yes of course you will,' answered Cherubino. 'We'll meet in the remote places, in the deep sea caverns, by the rocks at high tide.'

He clasped Valerie's hands again, but his touch was curiously cold, like marble. The moonlight was still playing over him but now it was making him flicker like lightning. He led Valerie to the high wall which overlooked the great garden beyond. The tops of the statues glimmered among the dense hedges. All at once Cherubino was on top of the wall looking down at her.

He looked very grand and beautiful.

'I won't tell anybody,' said Valerie, 'about you being a sea god, I mean. Not even Mama. And certainly not Miss McKenzie. She would never understand!'

Cherubino was poised to jump.

Then he turned back.

'By the way, sea gods can love humans sometimes, you know. Now and again – every thousand years or so. A very unusual human that is. And when we do, we have very long memories. Goodbye, Valerie, till we meet again.'

A cloud came over the moon. When it passed, Cherubino was gone.

VALERIE stood there trembling for a long time. At last she remembered that she was out in the garden in her nightdress, in the middle of the night. Very slowly she went back indoors and upstairs to bed. She lay wide awake, staring into the darkness.

AFTER this, life went on as usual; the flat days, the stifling routine. Nobody guessed that inside Valerie's head everything was different. She did her morning lessons with Miss McKenzie, as before, and in the afternoons they took their walk in the gardens.

One day they found that a change had been made. Cherubino's dolphin had disappeared. In its place was a graceful nymph with bound-up hair and trailing seaweed. She was very beautiful, but Valerie could not bear to look at her.

IT was a hot afternoon. When Miss McKenzie was settled on her favourite seat and, still sitting primly upright, had fallen into a light doze, Valerie escaped.

She wandered all alone (Mama would never have approved) through the maze of shaded walks, which criss-crossed one another like a giant's ruled-out pattern book, venturing further than ever before.

HIGH up, where the last hedge of the gardens met the steep hillside, the paths became more overgrown. There was a flight of shallow stone steps, now cracked and neglected, with a channel running down the centre where water had once tumbled. Now the fountain at the top was dried up and covered with moss and ferns.

Valerie climbed the steps and peered into the shade beyond.

THIS was where the gardeners
tipped their grass cuttings and
stacked the plant pots and
cracked urns. Scattered in the
long grass were bits of statues,
stone legs and arms, grinning
dragons split apart by time and
heads of Roman emperors
who had long since lost their
bodies. And there, dumped
down high and dry among
them, was the dolphin. He
seemed lonely and abandoned,
but he was still smiling his
wide dolphin smile.

VALERIE hurried over and knelt down in front of him. She stroked his domed forehead and ran her fingers along his wide jaws. She looked into his stone eyes and he looked back at her.

It was a meeting of long lost friends. And for the first time in so many dreary days, Valerie smiled.

It was as though they both knew for sure, now, that they were going to find Cherubino again. Or, he would find them.

SOMEWHERE, where remote caverns fill up with lapping water at high tide, and spray foams against the rocks, and breakers roll in endlessly along the beach, and the shining swell is moving, moving far out towards the sky… There, one day, as Cherubino had promised, they would meet again.

More Red Fox picture books
for you to enjoy

MUMMY LAID AN EGG
by Babette Cole

RUNAWAY TRAIN
by Benedict Blathwayt

DOGGER
by Shirley Hughes

WHERE THE WILD THINGS ARE
by Maurice Sendak

OLD BEAR
by Jane Hissey

MISTER MAGNOLIA
by Quentin Blake

ALFIE GETS IN FIRST
by Shirley Hughes

OI! GET OFF OUR TRAIN
by John Burningham

GORGEOUS
by Caroline Castle and Sam Childs